Author's Note

In 1898 Joshua Slocum became the first man to sail around the world alone. On the sloop *Spray*, which he rebuilt himself from an old oyster sloop and the timber of other ships, he sailed for three years, two months, and two days and had a lifetime of experiences. He sailed through seas fair and ferocious. He fought pirates off Gibraltar and barbarians off South America. Slocum claimed the ghost of the pilot of Columbus' *Pinta* sailed *Spray* for him when he got sick from eating plums and white cheese.

After his remarkable voyage, Joshua Slocum struggled for ten years to fit into the ways of the world. Finally, on November 14, 1909, Captain Slocum put his belongings aboard *Spray* and sailed out of Martha's Vineyard, never to be seen again.

The people of the Vineyard didn't forget Slocum. They puzzled and wondered and always expected the hearty Slocum to sail again along their shore.

Spray

Robert J. Blake

Philomel Books

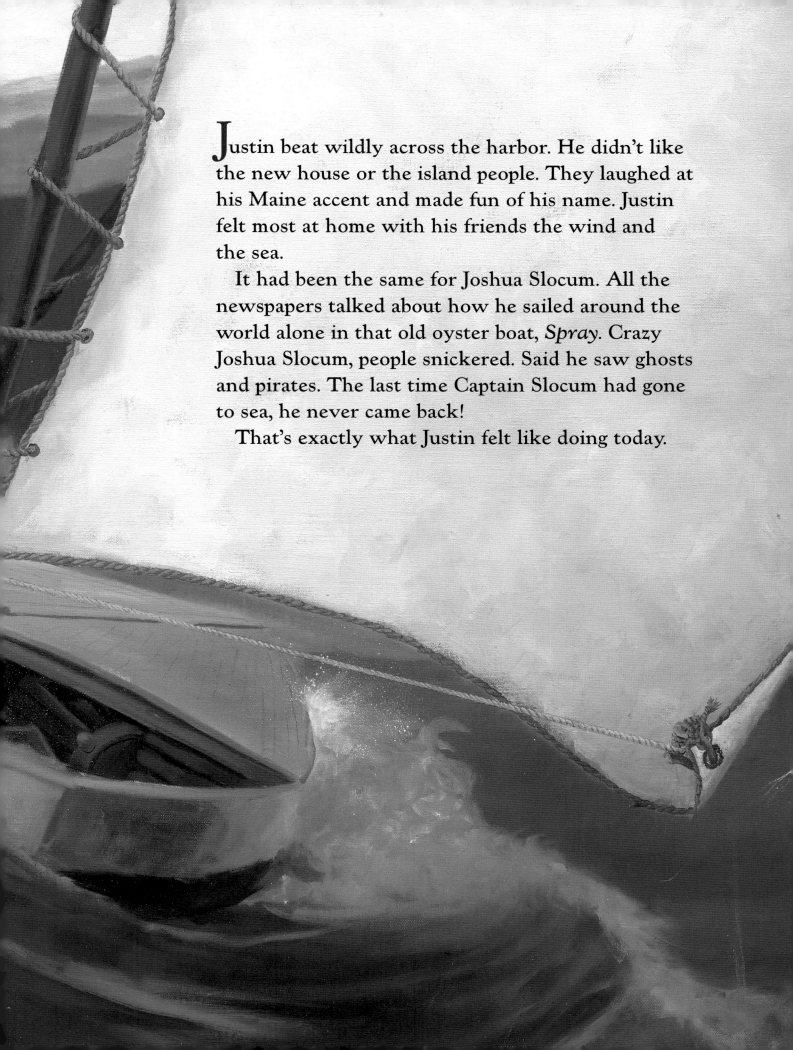

Justin beat wildly across the harbor. He didn't like the new house or the island people. They laughed at his Maine accent and made fun of his name. Justin felt most at home with his friends the wind and the sea.

It had been the same for Joshua Slocum. All the newspapers talked about how he sailed around the world alone in that old oyster boat, *Spray*. Crazy Joshua Slocum, people snickered. Said he saw ghosts and pirates. The last time Captain Slocum had gone to sea, he never came back!

That's exactly what Justin felt like doing today.

Justin cut by the Two Sisters bouys and far past where the sea begins to build. With the wind at his back, he challenged the sea. Just like Joshua Slocum.

But the wind caught him daydreaming and conspired with the sea. Together they tangled him in his sails and dumped him into the water.

"Here's a sailor's got himself tangled up in things," said a rough voice as Justin came to the surface. A firm hand pulled him onto an old sloop.

The bowsprit was crooked and the planking mismatched. She needed a good going-over.

So did the man. He wore a battered hat, his trousers were unbuttoned, and his boots were laced all wrong.

"*Spray*," Justin heard himself whisper. "*Captain Slocum*."

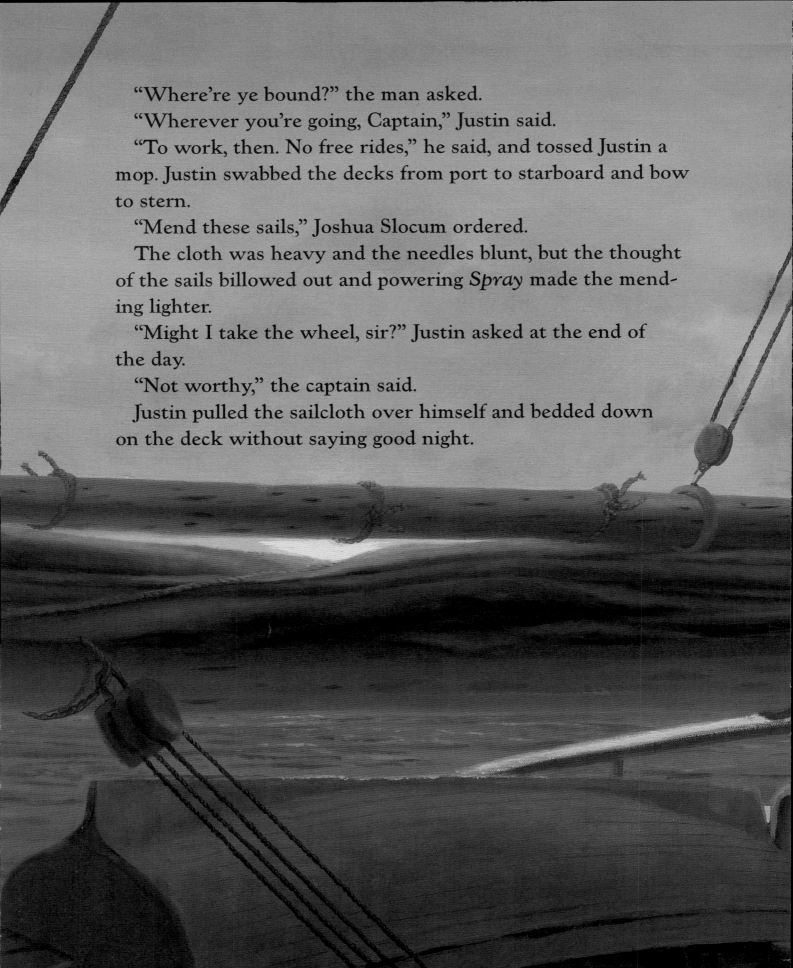

"Where're ye bound?" the man asked.

"Wherever you're going, Captain," Justin said.

"To work, then. No free rides," he said, and tossed Justin a mop. Justin swabbed the decks from port to starboard and bow to stern.

"Mend these sails," Joshua Slocum ordered.

The cloth was heavy and the needles blunt, but the thought of the sails billowed out and powering *Spray* made the mending lighter.

"Might I take the wheel, sir?" Justin asked at the end of the day.

"Not worthy," the captain said.

Justin pulled the sailcloth over himself and bedded down on the deck without saying good night.

A screaming sea hammered *Spray* in the morning.

"Batten down the main hatch," Slocum shouted across the wind. "Tend the lines." Justin closed the hatch and tended the ropes.

All day they fought through the storm. All day Justin carried out Slocum's bidding. *Spray* quarreled with the sea, rolling the whitecaps under. When the wind turned, Joshua tied off the wheel and ran forward to set the jib sail.

"Should I take the wheel, sir?" Justin shouted across the wind.

"Not worthy," the captain said.

Justin found some plums and cheese in a bowl. "Don't eat them!" barked the captain. But Justin ate everything in spite of him and curled into the sailcloth for the night.

Justin awoke in the middle of the night. The sea was still pounding. Slocum was asleep across the cabin. A giant of a man was at the helm.

"Take the wheel," the stranger said.

Was it the cheese, the green plums? *Or was this one of Slocum's ghosts?*

Justin took the wheel.

"Set your footing," said the stranger.

Spray caught the wind and flew over the waves. *He had her.*

Until *Spray* heeled under his hand.

"She won't come up!" the boy shouted.

"Let the mainsail out," the stranger roared.

Justin strained to let the sail out. The line ripped through his hands and the boom swung out of control. The captain jumped up and took the wheel.

"Douse the main," he ordered.

Justin obeyed. The stranger was gone.

The morning broke fair and calm. Set upon the cabin top was a breakfast of butter and biscuits and tea.

"Eat hearty," said the captain. "Ye'll have a go at the wheel today."

Justin was eating quickly when a parrot swooped down out of nowhere.

Where did he come from? thought Justin.

"Bad omen," said the captain.

Now Justin took the wheel in a fair wind.

"Head up to starboard," ordered the captain.

Justin turned the wheel.

"Steady as she goes," the captain said.

"Steady."

"Drifting to windward," Slocum warned.

Justin threw *Spray* back to leeward…

too far!

So he swung her the other way…

too far!

And back again…too far! No matter what Justin did, *Spray* went her own way.

Joshua Slocum's hands covered his. "Easy, now," he said. "Don't fight her. Work with her."

"Work with her," the wind whispered.

Slowly, Justin began to feel *Spray* under his hands. She worked with the water, defied the water, and knew when to give herself to a sure hand at the wheel.

As the sun sat on the horizon, Justin wished the day would never end.

That night set gently. *Spray* felt like an island on the sea.
Justin and Joshua Slocum stared at the stars.

"I used to think they were holes in the night sky,"
Justin said.

"What matters is that they help us stay our course," the
captain said.

"What is our course?"

Slocum didn't answer.

"The other side," came a voice on a breeze.

Justin wondered.

"*Spray* is a fine ship, Captain."

"A wise ship, Justin. Old and wise. Made of the timber of
many ships. A sloop, a cutter, a ketch, even a schooner. She's
been many ships to many people."

"I did well today, sir."

"Fair. You did fair."

The morning crept in with a fog thick enough to stand on. "Captain?" Justin called. "Captain?"

Only the wind answered him. The seas were picking up again, the sails flapping.

Justin ran to the stern, but the captain was not to be seen. He peered over the rail, then dropped to the deck.

There, rising out of the fog as though riding on a cloud, was a towering man-of-war. A pirate ship!

The ropes set themselves. *Spray*'s sails flew open. Justin took the helm.

"Work with her," he whispered to himself.

Spray came alive in his hands. She leapt on the waves. But when Justin looked back, the black-sailed ship was on them.

"Run, *Spray*!" Justin shouted. But the old oyster sloop was not made for any chase.

"Old and wise," whispered the wind.

"Many ships to many people," called the sea. Justin understood.

Justin set his feet. "Sail yourself, *Spray*," he shouted. "Be all the ships you've ever been."

Spray became all the ships she had ever been.

As though the wind and sea were theirs to command, they out-sailed the black-sailed schooner.

Spray and Justin were alone again on the sea.

"Captain!" Justin called. "What will be our heading?"

"Your command," came a voice.

"Then to home." Justin turned. "And for those who would be coming, there will be no free ride."

"We won't be coming," whispered the wind.

"We are already home," called the sea.

"Come back!" shouted Justin.

But he shouted from his own dory. The wind caught his words and the sea led his bow.

It is always harder to get home than it is to run away. Justin held fast.

To my pilot,
Patricia Lee Gauch.

A very special thank you to Harden and Ailsa Crawford.

Copyright © 1996 by Robert Blake

Philomel Books, a division of The Putnam & Grosset Group,
200 Madison Avenue, New York, NY 10016.
Philomel Books, Reg. U.S. Pat. & Tm. Off.
Published simultaneously in Canada.
Printed in Hong Kong by South China Printing Co. (1988) Ltd.
Book design by Patrick Collins. The text is set in Kennerley Medium.

Library of Congress Cataloging-in-Publication Data
Blake, Robert J. Spray / Robert Blake. p. cm.
Summary: At home with the wind and the sea, Justin sails his dory
across the harbor and suddenly finds himself in the company of the
legendary Captain Slocum aboard the Spray.
1. Slocum, Joshua, b. 1844—Juvenile Fiction. [1. Slocum, Joshua
b. 1844—Fiction. 2. Spray (Sloop)—Fiction. 3. Sailing—Fiction.] I. Title.
PZ7.B564Sp 1996 [Fic]—dc20 94-32514 CIP AC   ISBN 0-399-22770-9

10 9 8 7 6 5 4 3 2 1

First Impression